OLAF'S AMAZING ADVENTURES

Three tales to enjoy...

Olaf's Perfect Summer Day

Olaf's New Reindeer Friend

Olaf and the Troll Tots

Bath • New York • Cologne • Melbourne • Delhi
Hong Kong • Shenzhen • Singapore • Amsterdam

OLAF's Perfect Summer Day

Summer had finally arrived in Arendelle. Everyone in the kingdom was enjoying the long, sunny days after a very cold winter season.

But today was going to be the hottest day of the year so far! Most of the villagers wanted to stay inside where it was cool.

But Olaf could hardly wait to get outside! This was the kind of day he had always dreamed about!

Olaf ran into Princess Anna's room, calling out happily. "Anna, Anna! Guess what today is! It's the perfect summery day! Let's go outside and play!"

Anna groaned as she sat up in bed. "It's too hot, Olaf!" But she had to smile when she saw Olaf's hopeful face.

Together, Olaf and Anna went to look for Queen Elsa. They found her in the Great Hall.

"There you are, Elsa!" Olaf cried out joyfully.

Olaf looked up shyly at the important-looking visitor who was standing with Elsa.

"Hi, my name is Olaf and I like warm hugs."

"H-h-hello," the visitor stammered in surprise. He had never seen a talking snowman before!

Olaf turned back to Elsa. "And today is the best day for warm hugs because it's sunny and hot. Please, can we go and play in the sunshine?"

Elsa laughed. "That sounds like fun, Olaf. What did you have in mind?"

"It's so hot, though," Anna interrupted. "Couldn't you cool things down just a bit, Elsa?" She looked hopefully at her sister.

"Olaf's always wanted to experience heat," said Elsa. "Shouldn't we give him his special day? We'll do everything he's always wanted to do in summer!"

"You're right, Elsa," agreed Anna. "How about a picnic on the shores of the fjord?"

Olaf clasped his hands with glee. "Oooh, I love picnics!"

Anna, Elsa and Olaf headed to the royal kitchen to collect some picnic supplies. They found the cook with her head in the icebox!

"Olina, what on earth are you doing?" asked Elsa.

The cook popped her head up. “Trying to keep cool. It’s so terribly hot!”

Olaf chuckled. “Did you bake cookies today?”

The cook shook her head. “Oh, it’s too hot for baking.”

Elsa glanced at Olaf. She didn’t want him to miss out. “How about an ice-cold lemonade instead?” she suggested.

Olaf was thrilled. “Oooh, I love lemonade!”

Olaf, Anna and Elsa set off for their picnic.

In the royal gardens, a few children were lying on the grass. Olaf didn't realize they were too hot to play games. He ran over to them, giggling happily.

"Hi, my name is Olaf. Don't you just love summer?" The children liked Olaf, so they joined him in chasing butterflies and blowing fuzz off dandelions.

Even Elsa and Anna couldn't resist joining in!

After a while, Anna plopped herself down on the grass. "Whew! I'm ready for our picnic!" she said.

Elsa agreed. "Yes, let's head to the docks. We can sail to the fjord."

Olaf, who had been chasing a bumblebee, stopped in his tracks. "We're going sailing? I've always wanted to try sailing!"

At the docks, Anna and Elsa chose a beautiful sailing boat. As they set sail, Olaf hummed a happy tune. He even got to steer the boat for a while!

When they reached the shore, Olaf couldn't sit still!

"Don't you just love the feeling of sand on your snow?" he squealed. "Let's make sand angels!"

Anna gingerly stuck a toe in the hot sand. "Oh, goodness, that is ... warm!" she cried.

Anna danced on tiptoe over the hot sand to the fjord's edge. "Ah, this is better," she said, as the cool water washed over her feet.

The three friends spent the whole afternoon playing in the summer sun.

They built sandcastles and sand people.

They chased waves on the shore
and even danced with seagulls!

And finally, when they'd tired themselves out, they sat down and had a wonderful picnic on the shores of the fjord.

"Hands down, this is the best day of my life," said Olaf.

As they sailed back to Arendelle, the setting sun made beautiful colours in the sky. Olaf was amazed. "I wish I could hug the summer sun. I bet it would feel wonderful!"

Anna smiled as she swept her sweaty hair off her face. "You might need a bigger snow flurry for that, Olaf!"

The trio soon reached the dock, where Kristoff and Sven were waiting to greet them. Everyone was tired after the hot day – apart from Olaf, who couldn't stop talking about the picnic!

"Summer is wonderful," Elsa said with a wink. "But tomorrow, I predict a chance of snow."

THE END

OLAF'S New Reindeer Friend

Princess Anna and Queen Elsa were working hard to prepare for the kingdom's first ball since Elsa's magical powers had been revealed. The people of Arendelle had accepted Elsa and her magic, and the sisters wanted to thank them with a special celebration.

"I want the people to know we care," Elsa said. "I want this ball to be different from anything they've ever seen!"

"Oh, Elsa," said Anna. "Just having a ball is special enough!"

"I agree, Your Majesty," said a servant, entering the room.

The kindly servant looked around. "Hmm ... crocus flowers would be nice for the centrepieces."

"That's true, but everything already looks beautiful," Anna said. "The party is tonight, Elsa, and you need a break. Besides, I want to spend some time with you!"

"I'd love to," replied Elsa. "But what about the crocuses?"

"Well," said Anna, thinking quickly, "let's gather them ourselves! We'll be doing something useful *and* spending time together."

"What a good idea!" said Elsa. "And Olaf can help, too."

Anna and Elsa found Olaf just outside the castle.

"Hello, Olaf!" said Anna. "We're going to look for crocuses. Will you help us?"

Olaf clapped his hands. "Ooooh! I love crocuses!"

Anna, Elsa and Olaf walked into the mountains and played all day long.

They enjoyed having fun outside of the castle walls!

"Maybe our party should be fancy dress!" Anna suggested, giggling.

"That's right, the ball!" said Elsa. She had almost forgotten about it. "Don't forget, we still need a lot more crocuses!"

As they walked further along the path, Anna spotted Wandering Oaken's Trading Post and Sauna.

"Look! I remember this place," cried Anna. "I bet Oaken will have something for our ball."

Olaf couldn't wait to see inside!

"Hoo-hoo!" called Oaken as they entered the shop.

"Hello! Do you have anything special for a ball?" asked Anna.

"My big winter blowout is special. Half price shoes for walking on snow! Or karts for sliding down mountains!" Oaken exclaimed.

Outside, Elsa looked at Anna's sledge full of shopping. "Those things aren't very useful for the ball," she said.

"I know," Anna grinned. "But he was so nice, how could I say no?"

Elsa laughed. As they set out again, Olaf ran ahead, shouting, "This is the best day of my life!"

Soon the group found lots more crocuses.

Elsa gasped. “They’re beautiful!”

While the girls collected flowers, Olaf chased a bee. All was well until ...

... Olaf nearly ran off the edge of a cliff!

"Hang on there, Olaf!" exclaimed Elsa, using her magic to stop him falling over the edge.

But Olaf didn't even notice. "Look at that!" he said, staring at something below. It was a young reindeer trapped on a ledge.

"How did you get down there?" Anna asked. "And how will we get you back up?"

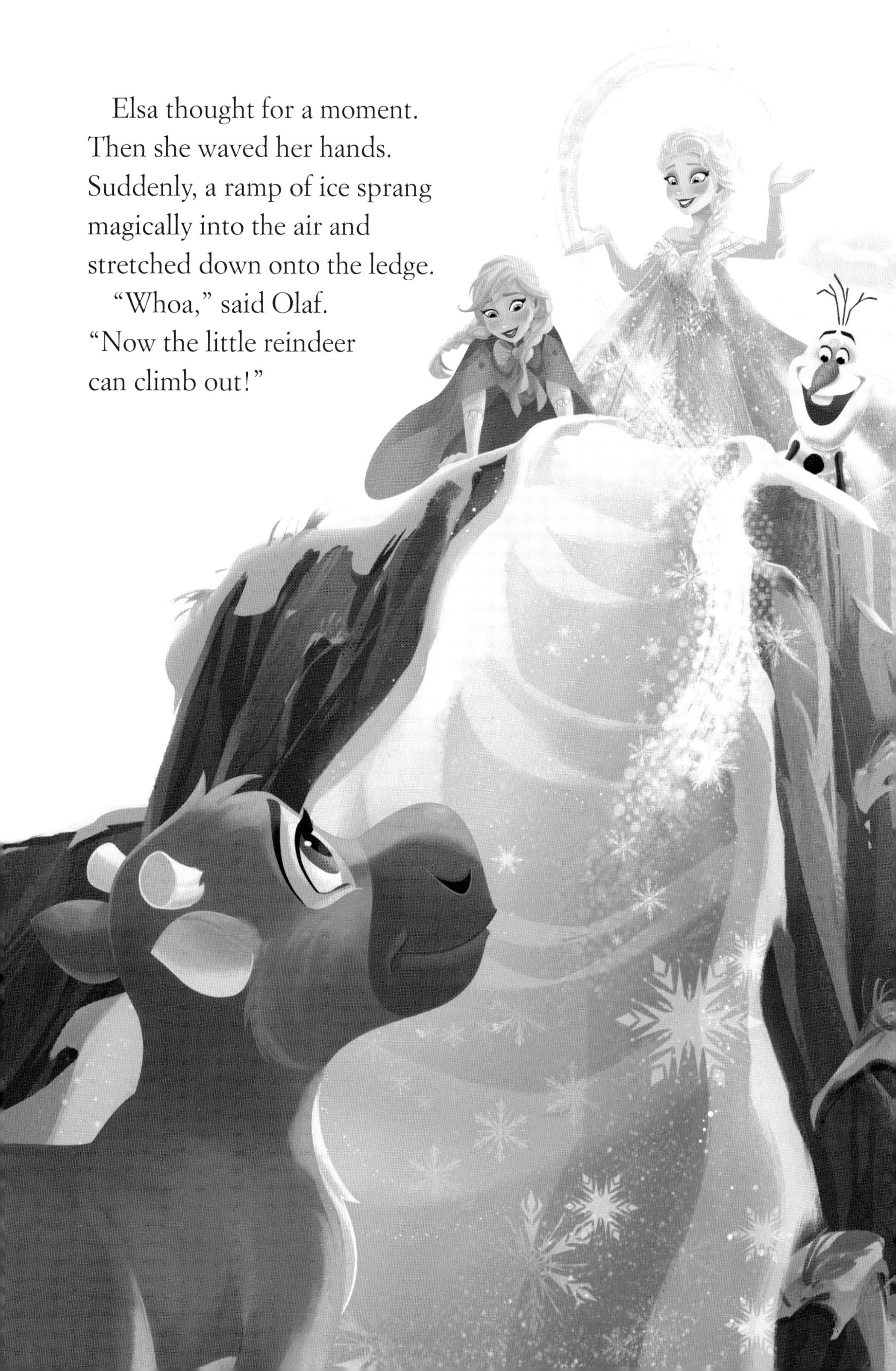

Elsa thought for a moment. Then she waved her hands. Suddenly, a ramp of ice sprang magically into the air and stretched down onto the ledge.

"Whoa," said Olaf. "Now the little reindeer can climb out!"

Carefully, the reindeer stepped on to the ice ramp ... but it was too slippery!

“Now what?” asked Elsa.

“I know!” said Anna. She grabbed the shopping she had bought at Oaken’s Trading Post, jumped onto the ramp and slid down to join the little reindeer on the ledge.

First, Anna pulled out the snowshoes. "I knew these would be useful," she said, fitting them on the reindeer.

Then she tied a rope round the reindeer and threw it to Elsa. "Pull!" Anna shouted.

Elsa and Olaf pulled on the rope together.

At last, everyone was safely at the top!

"Can we invite the reindeer to the ball?" asked Olaf.

"The ball!" Anna and Elsa shouted together. They needed to get back to the castle!

Elsa grabbed Anna's and Olaf's hands and led them to the kart. "Hold on!" she said. Using her magic, Elsa created snow slide after snow slide, and they slid all the way down the mountain.

When they arrived at the palace, Elsa, Anna, Olaf and the little reindeer landed right in the middle of the ballroom!

Crocus flowers rained down on the guests, who were delighted by the grand entrance.

“See?” said Anna. “Nobody has ever seen a ball like this before!” Elsa laughed. “And best of all, we’re all enjoying it together!”

THE END

OLAF
and the Troll Tots

Anna, Kristoff and Sven were heading towards the setting sun. They were off to Troll Valley to babysit the toddler trolls while the adults went to their annual magic convention.

"I wonder if I should have brought games," Anna said. "Do trolls like games?"

"Oh, don't worry," Kristoff replied. "They'll probably be sleeping the whole time. I bet we'll just be relaxing by the fire and maybe eating some snacks."

He explained that Bulda, his adoptive troll mother, had a very strict bedtime for all the young trolls. Sven grunted in agreement.

They reached Troll Valley and were greeted warmly by the trolls.

"It seems like just yesterday you were young enough to have a babysitter yourself, Kristoff," said Bulda. "All you wanted to do was run naked through the valley!"

"Oh, really?" Anna asked, stifling a giggle.

"Okay, that's enough stories for now," Kristoff said.

Bulda took Anna and Kristoff to the troll tots.

"If they get hungry, you can feed them smashed berries. And they may need a leaf change. But it's just about their bedtime, so they should be sleeping soon."

As the adult trolls headed off, Anna waved goodbye. "Have a great time! Everything is going to be fine...."

But everything wasn't fine!

As soon as the adult trolls left, the toddlers escaped from their pen. They were running, climbing and swinging all over the place!

"Oh no, no," Anna said, rushing to help a few tots who were climbing the boulders. "That's dangerous."

Kristoff ran to a leaning tower of troll tots that had just sprouted.

"All right, guys," Kristoff said, gently pulling the trolls off one another. "Let's settle down now."

But the more that Kristoff and Anna tried to calm the little trolls, the wilder they became!

"Maybe they're hungry!" Anna said, heading for the basket of smashed berries.

"Yummy!" she cooed. But the trolls clearly felt they had better things to do.

"Maybe they need changing?" Kristoff said, bravely peering into one of the trolls' nappy leaves. "Nope!"

"Let's put them to bed," Anna suggested. "They must be tired by now."

But the young trolls were wide awake.

Suddenly, a cheery voice interrupted them.
"Hello, troll babies!"
It was Olaf!

"Elsa sent me in case you needed some help," Olaf explained as the tots clambered all over him. "Why, hi there. Ha ha! That tickles!" Olaf was a real hit with the little trolls!

"Boy, are we glad to see you," Kristoff said.

Anna ran to greet the snowman. But in her hurry, she tripped, falling face-first into the basket of berries!

"Whoaaa!" she yelled.

Kristoff rushed to her side. "Anna! Are you okay?"

Anna lifted her head, her face covered in dripping purple goop.

The little trolls burst into loud giggles. They leaped up and started lapping up the berry juice from her cheeks!

Anna laughed. "Well, I guess that's one way to feed them."

After the trolls had finished all the berry juice, they sat in a row, happy and full. But suddenly, a strange smell floated into the air. The trolls looked down at their leaves.

"Uh-oh," Kristoff said, realizing what had happened. "Olaf, you distract them."

Olaf happily told the little trolls stories about his favourite thing in the world – summer. Anna and Sven collected new leaves while Kristoff changed the nappies. Soon everyone was clean and sweet-smelling once more!

"And now for my show-stopping song about summer!" Olaf announced.

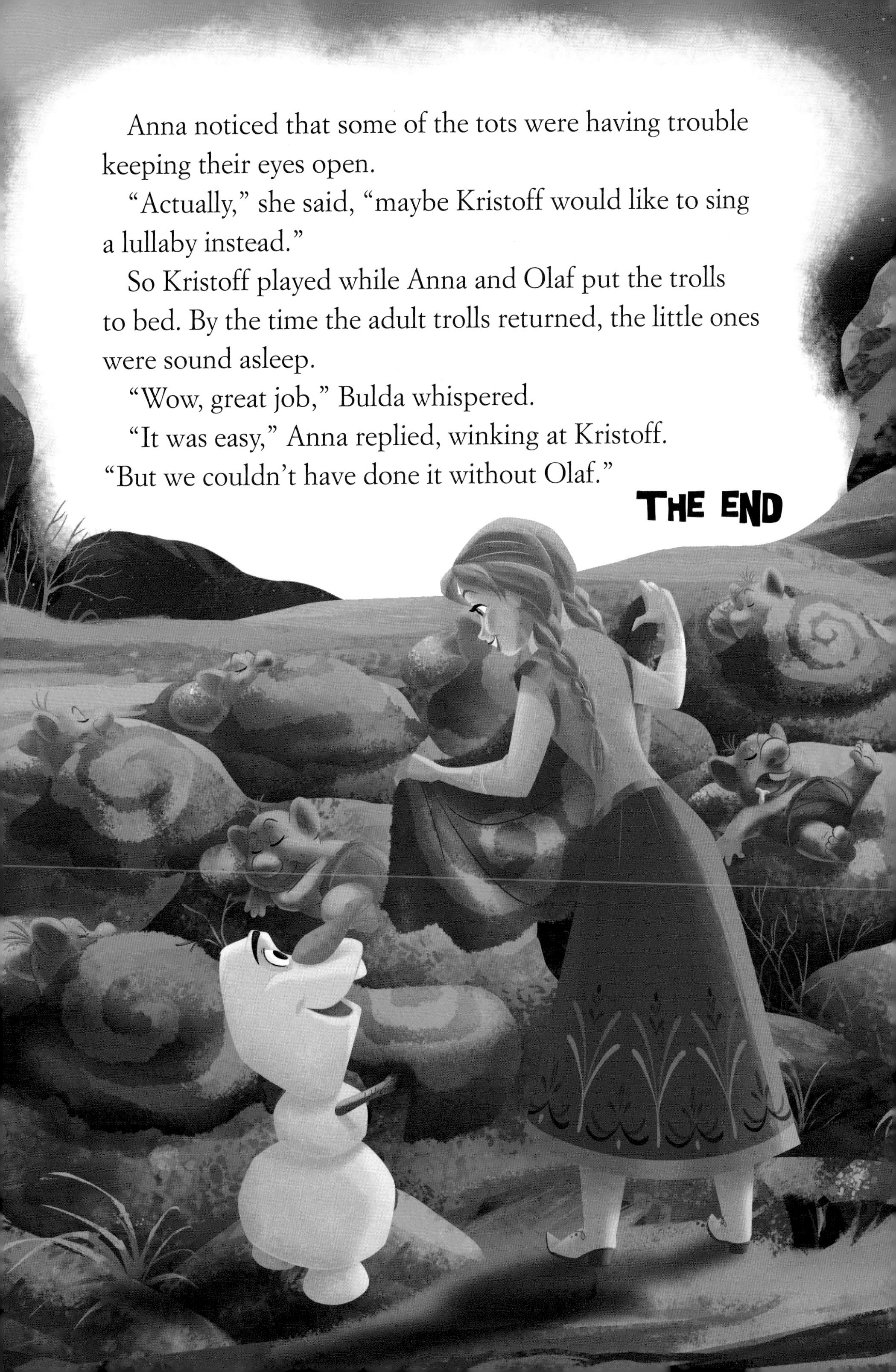

Anna noticed that some of the tots were having trouble keeping their eyes open.

"Actually," she said, "maybe Kristoff would like to sing a lullaby instead."

So Kristoff played while Anna and Olaf put the trolls to bed. By the time the adult trolls returned, the little ones were sound asleep.

"Wow, great job," Bulda whispered.

"It was easy," Anna replied, winking at Kristoff. "But we couldn't have done it without Olaf."

THE END